The Secret Princess

and other princess stories

Compiled by Tig Thomas

Miles KeLLY

First published in 2013 by Miles Kelly Publishing Ltd
Harding's Barn, Bardfield End Green, Thaxted, Essex, CM6 3PX, UK

This edition printed 2014

2 4 6 8 10 9 7 5 3

Publishing Director Belinda Gallagher
Creative Director Jo Cowan
Editorial Director Rosie Neave
Senior Editor Claire Philip
Senior Designer Joe Jones
Production Manager Elizabeth Collins
Reprographics Stephan Davis, Jennifer Cozens, Thom Allaway
Assets Lorraine King

ISBN 978-1-78209-217-9

Printed in China
British Library Cataloguing-in-Publication Data
A catalogue record for this book is available from the British Library

ACKNOWLEDGEMENTS
The publishers would like to thank the following artists who have contributed to this book:
Smiljana Coh, Mélanie Florian, Kirsten Wilson, Jennie Poh, Karen Sapp (cover)

All other artwork from the Miles Kelly Artwork Bank

The publishers would like to thank the following sources for the use of their photographs:
Cover frame: Karina Bakalyan/Shutterstock.com
Inside frame: asmjp/Shutterstock.com

Made with paper from a sustainable forest
www.mileskelly.net   info@mileskelly.net

Contents

The Shepherdess

By Paul Sébillot

ONCE UPON A TIME there lived a king who had two daughters. He loved them both very much. When they grew up, he made up his mind that he would give his kingdom to the one who could best show how much she loved him.

So he called the eldest princess and said to her, "How much do you love me?"

"You are the apple of my eye," she said.

"Ah!" exclaimed the king, "you are indeed a good daughter."

Then he sent for the younger daughter, and asked her how much she loved him.

"I love you, my father," she answered, "as I love the salt in my food."

This made the king very angry for salt seemed a very little thing to him, and he ordered her to leave the court, and never appear before him again. The poor princess made a bundle of her jewels and her best dresses and hurriedly left the castle where she was born.

She walked away, without knowing what was to become of her, for she had never been shown how to work. And as she was afraid that no one would want to hire a girl with such a pretty face, she decided to make herself as ugly as she could.

She took off her royal dress and put on some horrible old rags belonging to a

beggar. After that she
smeared mud all over
her hands and face,
and shook her hair into
a great tangle. After
walking for a great many
days she came to a
neighbouring kingdom. She
arrived at a large farm where
they needed a shepherdess, and
were glad to hire her.

One day when she was watching her
sheep in a lonely part of the country, she
felt a wish to dress herself in her robes of
splendour. She washed herself in the stream
and put on her fine robes, which she always
carried with her. The king's son, who had
lost his way out hunting, saw her from a
distance, and wished to look at her closer.

But the girl sped into the wood as swiftly as
a bird. When she was quite safe, she put on
her rags again, and smeared mud over
her face and hands. However the
young prince, who was both
hot and thirsty, found his way
to the farm to ask for a drink,
and he asked the name of
the beautiful lady that
looked after the sheep.

At this everyone began
to laugh, for they said
that the shepherdess was
one of the ugliest and
dirtiest creatures under
the sun.

The prince thought
some witchcraft must be
at work, and he went away

before the return of the shepherdess.

But the prince thought often of the lovely maiden. At last he dreamed of nothing else, and grew thinner day by day until his parents promised to do all they could to make him as happy as he once was. He dared not tell them the truth, so he only said that he should like some bread baked by the shepherdess from the distant farm.

The maiden showed no surprise at receiving such an order, but merely asked for some flour, salt and water. Before beginning her work she washed herself carefully, and even put on her rings. While she was baking, one of her rings slid into the dough. When she had finished she dirtied herself again so that she became as ugly as before.

The loaf was brought to the king's son, who ate it with pleasure. But in it he found the ring of the princess, and declared to his parents that he would marry the girl whose finger that ring fitted.

So the king made a proclamation through his whole kingdom and ladies came from afar to win the prince. But the ring was so tiny that even those who had the smallest hands could only get it on their little fingers. In a short time all the maidens of the kingdom had tried on the ring. The king was just about to announce that their efforts had been in vain, when the prince said he had not yet

9

seen the shepherdess. They sent for her, and she arrived covered with rags, but with her hands cleaner than usual, so that she could easily slip on the ring.

The king's son declared that this was the girl he would marry. When his parents remarked that the girl was only a keeper of sheep the maiden said that she was born a princess, and that, if they would give her some water and leave her alone in a room for a few minutes, she would show them. They did what she asked, and when she entered in a magnificent dress, she looked so beautiful that all believed her. The king's son asked if she would marry him. The princess then told her story, and asked to invite her father to the wedding.

It was with great joy that the princess's father heard that she was alive and that a prince asked her hand in marriage. He had been deeply sorry for his hard words to her, and he hurried to be at the ceremony.

At the wedding feast they served her father bread without salt, and meat without seasoning. Seeing him eat very little, his daughter asked if he liked his food.

"No," he replied, "the dishes are carefully cooked, but they are all so tasteless."

"Did I not tell you, my father, that salt was the best thing in life?"

The king hugged his daughter, and begged her forgiveness. Then, for the rest of the wedding feast they gave him bread made with salt, and dishes with seasoning, and he said they were the best he had ever eaten.

The Mother and the Daughter who Worshipped the Sun

By Flora Annie Steele

ONCE UPON A TIME there lived a mother and a daughter who worshipped the Sun. Though they were very poor, they never forgot to honour the Sun, giving everything they earned to it except two small cornmeal cakes — one of which the mother ate, while the other was the daughter's share. Every day one cake apiece, and that was all.

Now it so happened that one day, when the mother was out at work, the daughter grew hungry, and ate her cake before dinnertime. Just as she had finished it a priest came by, and begged for some bread. So the daughter broke off half of her mother's piece and gave it to the priest in the name of the Sun.

By and by the mother returned, very hungry for her dinner, and lo and behold there was only half a cake left.

"Where is the remainder of the bread?" she asked.

"I ate my share of the cake," said the daughter, "and just as I finished, a priest came begging, so I was obliged to give him your half."

"A fine story!" said the mother, in a rage.

The Mother and the Daughter who Worshipped the Sun

"I believe you gave my cake in order to save yours!"

The daughter protested that she really had finished her cake before the priest came begging. She promised to give her mother her share the next day. But her mother told her to leave home, saying, "I will have no greedyguts in my house!"

So the daughter wandered away into the wild, crying. When she had gone a long, long way, she became very tired and climbed into a pipal tree for safety. She still cried while she rested among the branches.

After a time, a young prince came to the tree and lay down to sleep. As he lay there, he looked so beautiful. The daughter could not keep her eyes

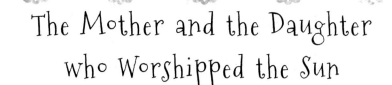

The Mother and the Daughter who Worshipped the Sun

off him, and so her tears flowed down onto him like a summer shower upon the young man's face. He woke with a start. Thinking it was raining, he rose to look at the sky, and see where this sudden storm had come from, but far and near not a cloud was to be seen. So he swung himself into the tree, and lo and behold, he found a beautiful maiden sitting in the tree, weeping sadly.

The Mother and the Daughter who Worshipped the Sun

"Where do you come from, fair stranger?" said he, and with tears in her eyes she told him she was homeless and motherless. He fell in love with her sweet face and soft words, so he asked her to be his bride, and she went with him to the palace, her heart full of gratitude to the Sun, who had sent her such good luck.

Everything she could desire was hers, but when the other women talked of their homes she held her tongue, for she was ashamed of hers.

Everyone thought she must be some great princess, she was so lovely and magnificent, but in her heart of hearts she knew she was nothing of the kind, so every day she prayed to the Sun that her mother might not find her out.

But one day, when she was sitting alone

in her beautiful palace, her mother appeared, ragged and poor as ever. She had heard of her daughter's good fortune, and had come to share it.

"And you shall share it," pleaded her daughter. "I will give you back far more than I ever took from you, if only you will not disgrace me before my prince."

"Ungrateful creature!" stormed the mother, "did you forget that it was through my act that your good fortune came to you? If I had not sent you out into the world, where would you have found so fine a husband?"

"I might have starved!" wept the daughter, "and now you come to destroy me again. Oh great Sun, help me now!"

Just then the prince came to the door, and the poor daughter was ready to die of shame and vexation, but when she turned to where her mother had sat, there was a magnificent golden stool.

"My princess," asked the prince, astonished, "where does that golden stool come from?"

"From my mother's house," replied the daughter, full of gratitude to the great Sun, who had saved her from disgrace.

"If there are such wonderful things to be seen in your mother's house," said the prince, "I must go and see it. Tomorrow we will set out on our journey, and you shall show me all it contains."

In vain the daughter put forward one excuse after another. The prince's curiosity had been aroused by the sight of the marvellous golden stool, and he was not to be put off.

Then the daughter cried once more to the great Sun, in her distress, saying, "Oh gracious Sun, help me now!"

But no answer came, and with a heavy heart she set out the next day to show the prince her mother's house. A fine procession they made, with horsemen and footmen clothed in royal liveries surrounding the coach, where the daughter sat, her heart sinking at every step.

And when they came close to where her mother's hut used to stand, there on the horizon was a shining, flaming golden palace that glittered and shone like solid sunshine. Within and without all was gold. A golden mother came out to greet them. She spoke graciously, for she remembered nothing about her trip to the prince's palace!

There they stayed, admiring the countless

marvels of the Sun palace for three days, and when the third day was over, the prince, more in love with his bride than ever, turned homewards. But when he came to the spot where he had first seen the glittering golden palace from afar, he thought he would take just one more look at the wondrous sight,

and lo, there was nothing to be seen except a low thatched hovel!

He turned to his bride, full of anger, and said, "You are a witch, and have tricked me! Confess, if you would not have me strike you dead!"

But the daughter fell on her knees, saying, "My gracious prince, believe me, I have done nothing! I am a poor homeless girl. I prayed to the Sun, and the Sun helped me!"

Then she told the whole story from beginning to end, and the prince was so well pleased that from that day he too worshipped the Sun.

The Secret Princess

A traditional Russian fairy tale

ONCE UPON A TIME there was a prince and princess who lived happily together. They loved each other very much and had nothing to worry them, but at last the prince grew restless. He longed to go out into the world to try his strength in battle against some enemy and win all kinds of honour.

So he called his army together and gave orders to start for a distant country where there ruled a cruel prince who ill-treated his subjects. The prince said goodbye to his beloved wife, and set off with his army across the seas.

I cannot say whether the voyage was short or long, but at last he reached the country and marched on, defeating all who came in his way. But this did not last long, for in time he came to a mountain pass, where a large army was waiting to take the prince himself prisoner.

He was captured easily, and carried off to prison and now our poor friend had a very bad time indeed. All night long the prisoners were chained up, and in the morning they were yoked together like oxen and had to plough the land till it grew dark. It was a miserable place.

This state of things went on for three years before the prince found any means of sending news of himself to his dear princess, but at last he managed to send this letter:

> *Sell all our castles and palaces, and then come and deliver me out of this horrible prison.*

The princess received the letter, read it, and wept bitterly as she said to herself, "How can I rescue my dearest husband?"

She thought, and at last an idea came to her. She cut off all her beautiful long brown hair and dressed herself in boy's clothes. Then she took her lute and went forth into the wide world. The princess travelled through many lands before she got to the town where the bad prince lived. When she got there she walked all round the palace and at the back she saw the prison.

Then she went into the great court in front of the palace, and taking her lute in her hand, began to play and sing as beautifully as she could.

When the cruel prince heard this touching song, sung by such a lovely voice, he had the singer brought before him.

"Welcome, O lute player," said he. "Where do you come from?"

"My country, sire, is far away across many seas," said the princess, "For years

I have been wandering about the world and gaining my living by my music."

The wicked prince replied, "Stay here a few days, and when you wish to leave I will give you what you ask for in your song — your heart's desire."

So the lute player stayed on in the palace and sang and played almost all day long to the prince.

After three days the lute player came to say goodbye to the prince.

"Well," said the prince, "what do you want as your reward?"

"Sire, give me one of your prisoners," she replied, "You have so many in your prison, and I should be glad of a companion on my journeys. When I hear his happy voice as I travel along I shall think of you."

"Come along then," said the prince,

"choose who you want." And he took the lute player through the prison himself.

The princess picked out her husband and although the cruel prince was not happy with her choice, she took him with her on her journey. Their journey lasted a great many days, but he never found out who she was, although he asked many times. Instead, the secret princess led him nearer to his own country.

When they reached the frontier the prisoner said, "Let me go now, kind lad. I am no common prisoner, but the prince of this country. Let me go free and ask what you will as your reward."

"Do not speak of reward now," said the lute player. "Go in peace." And so they parted ways. The princess took a short way home, got there before the prince and changed her dress. An hour later all the people in the palace were running to and fro and crying out with great excitement, "Our prince has come back! Our prince has returned to us!"

The prince greeted everyone kindly, but he would not so much as look at the princess. Then he called all his council and ministers together and said to them, "See what sort of a wife I have. She is happy to see me, but when I was pining in prison, she did nothing to help me."

And his council had to agree — they answered, "Sire, when news was brought from you the princess disappeared and no one knew where she went. She only returned to us today."

The prince was very angry indeed with the princess. He cried, "Why, you would never have seen me again, if a young lute player had not rescued me. I shall remember him with gratitude as long as I live."

Whilst the prince was sitting with his council, the princess put on her travelling cloak to disguise herself again. She took her lute, and slipping into the court sang, clear and sweet.

As soon as the prince heard this song he ran out to meet the lute player, took him by the hand and led him into the palace.

"Here," he cried, "is the boy who released me from my prison. And now, my true friend, ask for anything and I will give you your heart's desire."

"Sir, I ask of you what I asked and got from the bad prince. But this time I don't mean to give up what I get. I want you!"

And as she spoke she threw off her cloak

and everyone saw it was the princess.

Who can tell how happy the prince was? He held a great feast for his whole kingdom, and everyone came and rejoiced with him for a week. I was there too, and ate and drank many good things. I shall not forget it as long as I live.

The Twelve Huntsmen

A traditional Spanish fairy tale

ONCE UPON A TIME there was a prince who was engaged to a princess whom he dearly loved. One day as he sat by her side feeling very happy, he received news that his father was lying at the point of death, and wanted to see him before his end.

So he said to his love, "Alas! I must go off and leave you, but take this ring and wear it as a remembrance of me, and when I am king I will return and fetch you home."

Then he rode off, and when he reached his father he found him very near death.

The sick king said, "Dearest son, I have wanted to see you again before my end. Promise me, I beg of you, that you will marry who I choose," and he then named the daughter of a nearby king. The prince was so sad that he could think of nothing but his father, and cried, "Yes, yes, dear father, whatever you desire shall be done." And then the king closed his eyes and died.

After the prince had been proclaimed king, he felt that he must keep the promise he had made to his father, so he sent to ask for the hand of the king's daughter, which was granted to him.

Now, his first love heard of this, and the thought of her lover's desertion made her so sad that she pined away and nearly died.

Her father said to her, "My dearest child, why are you so unhappy? If there is anything you wish for, say so, and you shall have it."

His daughter thought for a moment, and then said, "Dear father, I wish for eleven girls as near as possible to my height, age and appearance."

So the king had his kingdom searched till eleven maidens of the same height, age and appearance as his daughter were found and brought to the palace.

Then the princess asked for twelve complete huntsmen's suits to be made, all exactly alike, and the eleven maidens had to dress themselves in eleven of the suits, while she herself put on the twelfth.

After this she said goodbye to her father, and rode off with her girls to the court of her former love. Here she enquired whether the king wanted some huntsmen, and if he would not take them all as his servants. The king saw her but did not recognize her, and said he would gladly hire them all. So they became the royal huntsmen.

Now, the king had a most remarkable lion, for it knew every hidden secret. One evening the lion said to the king, "You think you have got twelve huntsmen?"

"Yes, certainly," said the king.

"There you are mistaken," said the lion, "they are twelve maidens."

"That cannot possibly be," replied the king, "how do you mean to prove that?"

"Just have a number of dried peas scattered over the floor of your chamber," said the lion, "and you will soon see. Men have a strong, firm tread, so that if they happen to walk over peas not one will stir, but girls trip and slip and slide, so that the peas roll all about."

Fortunately one of the king's servants had become very fond of the young huntsmen, and he went to them and said, "The lion wants to persuade the king that you are only girls," and he told them all the plot.

The princess thanked him, and after he was gone she said to her maidens, "Make every effort to tread firmly on the peas."

Next morning, when the king sent for his twelve huntsmen, and they passed through the chamber — which was plentifully strewn with peas — they trod so firmly and walked with such a steady step that not one pea moved. After they were gone the king said to the lion, "There now — you have been telling lies — you see they walk like men."

"Because they knew they were being put to the test," answered the lion, "and so they made an effort. Have a dozen spinning-wheels placed in the chamber. When they pass through you'll see how interested they will be, quite unlike any man."

But the good-natured servant went to the huntsmen and told them this fresh plot. Then, as soon as the princess was alone with her maidens, she exclaimed, "Now, make sure you don't even look at those spinning-wheels."

When the king sent for his twelve huntsmen next morning they walked through the chamber without even casting a glance at the spinning-wheels.

The king said once more to the lion, "Why, you have deceived me again — they are men, for they never once looked at the spinning-wheels."

So the twelve huntsmen continued to follow the king, and he grew daily fonder of them. One day whilst they were all out hunting the news was brought that the king's intended bride was on her way.

When the true bride heard of this she felt as though a knife had pierced her heart, and she fell fainting to the ground. The king ran up to help, and began drawing off his gloves. Then he saw the ring that he had given to his first love, and as he gazed into her face he knew her again. His heart was so touched that he kissed her, and as she opened her eyes, he cried, "I am yours and you

are mine, and there is no power on earth that can alter that."

To the other princess he sent a messenger to beg her to return to her own kingdom. "For," said he, "I have a wife, and he who finds an old key does not need a new one."

And so the wedding was celebrated with great joy, and the lion was the chief guest, for after all he had told the truth.

Princess Peony

and other princess stories

Compiled by Tig Thomas

Miles Kelly

First published in 2013 by Miles Kelly Publishing Ltd
Harding's Barn, Bardfield End Green, Thaxted, Essex, CM6 3PX, UK

Copyright © Miles Kelly Publishing Ltd 2013

This edition printed 2014

2 4 6 8 10 9 7 5 3

Publishing Director Belinda Gallagher
Creative Director Jo Cowan
Editorial Director Rosie Neave
Senior Editor Claire Philip
Senior Designer Joe Jones
Production Manager Elizabeth Collins
Reprographics Stephan Davis, Jennifer Cozens, Thom Allaway
Assets Lorraine King

ISBN 978-1-78209-215-5

Printed in China

British Library Cataloguing-in-Publication Data
A catalogue record for this book is available from the British Library

ACKNOWLEDGEMENTS
The publishers would like to thank the following artists who have contributed to this book:
Marcin Piwowarski, Jennie Poh, Kirsten Wilson, Mélanie Florian, Helen Rowe (cover)

All other artwork from the Miles Kelly Artwork Bank

The publishers would like to thank the following sources for the use of their photographs:
Cover frame: Karina Bakalyan/Shutterstock.com
Inside frame: asmjp/Shutterstock.com

Made with paper from a sustainable forest
www.mileskelly.net   info@mileskelly.net

Contents

Noel's Princess

An extract from
The Story of the Treasure Seekers
by E Nesbit

SHE HAPPENED QUITE ACCIDENTALLY. We were not looking for a princess at all just then, but Noel had said he was going to find a princess all by himself — and he really did.

Greenwich Park is a jolly good place to play in, especially the parts that aren't near Greenwich. I often wish the park was nearer our house, but I suppose a park is a difficult thing to move.

The day the princess happened was a fine hot day, last October, and we were quite tired with the walk up to the park. When we'd rested a little, Alice said, "I see the white witch bear among the trees! Let's track it and slay it in its lair."

"I am the bear," said Noel, so he crept away, and we followed him among the trees. Often the witch bear was out of sight, and you didn't know where it would jump out from. Sometimes it just followed.

We hunted the bear in and out of the trees, and then we lost him altogether. Suddenly we found the wall of the park. Noel wasn't anywhere about. There was a door in the wall and it was open, so we went through.

We went over the stones on tiptoes, and found another wall with another door on the other side. We went through that too, on tiptoes. It really was an exciting adventure.

There was Noel. He was standing looking at a little girl — and she was the funniest little girl you ever saw.

She was just like a doll, with a pale face, and long yellow hair done up in two pigtails. Her cheeks came high up, like little shelves under her eyes. Her eyes were small and blue and she had on a funny black frock. As we came up near to them we heard her say to Noel, "Who are you?"

"I'm Prince Camaralzaman."

The funny little girl looked pleased.

"I thought at first you were a common boy," she said. Then she saw the rest of us and said, "Why, are you princesses and princes too?"

Of course we each said, "Yes," and she said, "I am a princess also."

She said it very well too, exactly as if it were the truth. We were very glad, because it is so seldom you meet any children who can begin to play a game straight away without having everything explained to them first.

This little girl had a funny voice — she didn't talk at all like we do.

Then we asked her name, and she went on and on, I thought she would never stop. The first were Pauline, Alexandra, Alice, and Mary was one, and Victoria, for we all heard that, and it ended with Hildegarde Cunigonde something or other, princess of something else.

When she'd done, Horace Octavius said, "Well that's jolly good! Say it again!" and she did. We told her our names, but she thought they were far too short, so when it was Noel's turn he said that he was called Prince Noel Camaralzaman Ivan Constantine Charlemagne James John Edward Biggs Maximilian Bastable Prince of Lewisham, but when she asked him to say it again of course he could only get the first two names right, because he had made it up on the spot as he went along.

So the princess said, "Why, you are old enough to know your own name. You should learn it off by heart."

She was very grave and serious. Then the strange little girl asked us where our maids and governesses were and we told her we hadn't any.

"How nice! Did you come here alone?"

"Yes," said Dora, "we came from across the heath."

"You are very fortunate," said the little girl. "I should like to go on the heath. There are donkeys there. I should like to ride them but my governess will not permit it, so I cannot go."

"Never mind that," said Noel, "I've got a lot of money. Come, let's go have a ride right now."

But the little girl shook her head and said she was afraid it would not be correct to go against her governess's wishes.

So instead we showed her how to play

cross-touch, and puss in the corner, and tag. She began to laugh at last and looked less like a doll. She was running after Dicky when suddenly she stopped short and looked as if she was going to cry. And we looked too, and there were two prim ladies with

little mouths and tight hair. One of them said, "Pauline, who are these children?"

The little girl said we were princes and princesses — which was silly, to a grown-up.

The lady gave a horrid laugh, and said, "Princes, indeed! They're common children!"

The little girl cried out, "Oh, I am so glad! When I am grown-up I'll always play with common children."

And she ran at us, and began to kiss us one by one, when the horrid lady said, "Your Highness go indoors at once!"

The little girl answered, "I won't!"

Then the prim lady said, "Wilson, carry her Highness indoors."

The little girl was carried away screaming, and between her screams she shrieked, "Common children! I am glad!"

The nasty lady then remarked to us,

"Now go, or I shall send for the police!"

So we all came away very quickly, and when we got outside Dora said, "So she really was a princess."

"And I thought it was play. And it was real. I wish I'd known! I should have liked to ask her lots of things," said Alice. Horace Octavius said he would have liked to ask her whether she had a crown.

So we all went home across the heath, and made toast. When we were eating Noel sighed, "I wish I could give her some toast." We knew he was thinking of the princess. He says now that she was as beautiful as the day, but we remember her well, and she was nothing of the kind.

Princess Peony

By Richard Gordon Smith

MANY YEARS AGO IN JAPAN, Princess Aya was walking in her garden with her maids-of-honour, just before her wedding. She wandered down through her favourite bed of peony flowers to the pond where she loved to gaze at her reflection on the nights of the full moon.

When she was near the pond her foot slipped, and she would have fallen into the water had it not been that a young man appeared as if by magic and caught her. She

Princess Peony

saw him briefly across the
water, then he disappeared.
The maids-of-honour had
seen her slip and a glimmer of
light but that was all.
But Princess Aya

had seen more. She had seen the most handsome young man she could imagine.

"Twenty-one years old," she said to her favourite maid, "he must have been a samurai of the highest order. His dress was covered with my favourite peonies. If only I could have seen him a minute longer, to thank him for saving me! Who can he be? And how could he have got into the palace gardens, through all the guards?"

After that evening Princess Aya fell sick. She could not eat or sleep, and turned pale. The wedding day came and went without the event — she was far too sick for that. As a last resource, her father sent for her favourite maid and demanded to know if she could give any reason for his daughter's mysterious sickness. Had she a secret love? Had she a dislike for her husband-to-be?

Her maid told him about the mysterious samurai. "Since that evening," she said, "our beloved Princess Aya has been sick, Sir. It is sickness of the heart. She is deeply in love with the young samurai she saw. There never was such a handsome man in the world before."

That evening the poor princess was more wearily unhappy than ever before. Thinking to enliven her a little, the maids sent for a celebrated musician.

The weather being hot, they were sitting on the balcony, and while the musician was playing, there appeared suddenly, from behind the peonies, the same handsome young samurai. He was visible to all this time —

even the peonies embroidered on his clothes could be seen.

"There he is! There he is!" cried the maids, at which he instantly disappeared again. The princess seemed more lively than she had been for days.

The next night, while two of the maids were playing music for their mistress, the figure of the young man appeared and disappeared once more. A thorough search was made in the immense peony flowerbeds with absolutely no result, not even the sign of a footprint.

A meeting was held, and it was decided by Princess Aya's father that a veteran officer of great strength and renown, Maki Hiogo, should try to capture the youth, should he appear again that evening. He arrived dressed in black to make him invisible in the dark night and hid himself among the peonies.

Music seemed to fascinate the young samurai. It was while music was being played that he had made his appearances. As the ladies played a piece called 'Sofuren', there, sure enough, arose the figure of a young samurai, dressed magnificently in clothes, which were covered with embroidered peonies.

Maki Hiogo stealthily approached the young man, and, seizing him around the waist, held him tight. But after a few seconds Maki Hiogo felt a kind of wet steam falling on his face. Still grasping the young samurai – for he had made up his mind that he would secure him – he fell to the ground.

As the guards rushed over to help, Maki

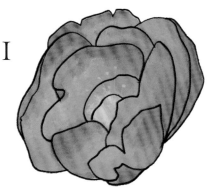

Hiogo shouted, "Come, gentlemen! I
have caught him. Come and see!"
But the man had disappeared, and
Maki Hiogo only held a large
peony in his arms!

By this time the king had arrived at the
spot where Maki Hiogo lay, and so had
Princess Aya and her maids-in-waiting.

All were astounded and mystified except
the king himself, who said "Ah! It is as I
thought. It is the spirit of the peony flower
that took the form of a prince."

Turning to his daughter and her maids, he
said, "You must take this as a great
compliment, and pay respect to the peony.
Show the one caught by Maki Hiogo
kindness by taking care of it."

So Princess Aya carried the flower back
to her room, where she put it in a vase of

water and placed it near her pillow. She felt as if she had her sweetheart with her.

Day by day she got better. She tended the peony herself, and, strangely, the flower seemed to get stronger and stronger, instead of fading.

At last the princess recovered. She became radiantly beautiful once again, while the peony continued to remain in perfect bloom, showing no sign of dying.

As Princess Aya was now perfectly well again, her father could no longer put off the wedding. Some days later, the bridegroom and all his family arrived at the castle, and the next day he was married to Princess Aya in a great ceremony.

As soon as the wedding was over, the peony was found dead and withered still in

its vase. After this, the
villagers called Princess Aya
'Princess Peony' instead.

The Swan Children of Lir

By Thomas Higginson

This is a story from Irish
folklore. Erin is a name for Ireland.
The name Aodh is pronounced 'Eh'.

KING LIR OF ERIN HAD FOUR YOUNG
children who were cared for by their
stepmother, the new queen, but there
came a time when she grew very jealous of
the love their father had for them.

Sometimes there was murder in the
stepmother's heart, but she could not bear
the thought of that wickedness, so she chose
another way to get rid of them.

One day she took the children for a drive in her chariot. There was Princess Finola, who was eight years old, and her three younger brothers — Aodh, Fiacre and little Conn, still a baby. They were beautiful children, with skin as white and soft as swans' feathers, and with large blue eyes and sweet voices.

Now, the wicked stepmother was of the magician's race, and she had magical powers. After they had journeyed for a short while they reached a large lake. The wicked stepmother told the four children that they could go and swim in the crystal clear water so they walked down to the lake and began swimming joyfully. Soon after, however, the queen took out her magic wand and cast a terrible spell.

One by one the children turned into four

beautiful, snow-white swans. The swans still had human voices, and so Finola said to the queen, "This wicked deed of yours will be punished one day. How long shall we be in the shape of swans?"

"For three hundred years on smooth Lake Darvra," said the queen, "then three hundred years on the Sea of Moyle, and then three hundred years at Inis Glora, in the Great Western Sea. Until St Patrick comes to Ireland, and you hear the bell, you shall not be freed. Neither your power nor mine can bring you back to human shape, but you shall keep your human reason and your speech, and you shall sing music so sweet that all who hear it shall listen."

She left them, and before long their father, King Lir, came to the shore and heard their singing. He asked how they came to have human voices.

"We are your four children, Father," said Finola, "changed into swans by our stepmother's jealousy."

"Then come and live with me," said her sorrowing father.

"We cannot leave the lake," she said, "or

live with our people anymore. But we are allowed to dwell together and to keep our reason and our speech, and to sing sweet music to you." So they sang to the king and his followers and lulled them to sleep.

When King Lir awoke he was determined to find his wife, the queen. He discovered she had returned to her father's palace and so the king journeyed there.

When he arrived, King Lir told the queen's father, King Bove, what the queen had done, and he was furious.

"This wicked deed," said King Bove, "shall punish the queen more than the innocent children, for their suffering shall end, but hers never shall."

King Bove asked the queen what bird, beast or devil she most hated, and she replied, "The demon of the air — the bat."

"So be it," said King
Bove, who also had
magical power. He
struck the queen
with his wand,
and she became
a bat. Legend says 'She is still a demon of
the air and shall be until the end of time'.

After this, people used to come to the lake
and listen to the swans. The happy were
made happier and the sad forgot their
sorrows. There was peace in all that region,
while war filled other lands. Vast changes
took place in three centuries but still the
swan-children lived, until at the end of three
hundred years they flew away to the stormy
Sea of Moyle. From then on it was the law
that no one should kill a swan in Erin.

Beside the Sea of Moyle they no longer

found the peaceful and
wooded shores they had
known, but rocky
coasts and wild water.
There came a great storm
one night, and the swans
knew that they could not
keep together. They resolved that if
separated they would meet at a rock called
Carricknarone. Finola arrived first, and took
her brothers under her wings. So passed their
lives until Finola sang one day, "The Second
Woe has passed — the second period of three
hundred years."

They flew out on the ocean, and went to
the island of Inis Glora. There they spent the

next three hundred
years amid wilder
storms and colder winds.

One May morning, as they floated in the
air around Inis Glora, they heard a faint bell
sounding across the eastern sea. They saw
beyond the waves, a priest, with attendants
around him on the Irish shore. They knew
that it must be St Patrick. Sailing through
the air towards their native coast, they
heard the bell once more and they knew
that all evil spirits were fleeing. As they
approached the land, St Patrick stretched out
his hand and said, "Children of Lir, you
may tread your native land again."

When they touched the shore, they
became human again, but they now
appeared old, pale and wrinkled.

And then they died, but, even as they did

so, a change swiftly came over them. They were children again, in their white night-clothes, as when their father King Lir, long centuries ago, had kissed them at evening. Their time of sorrow was over, but the cruel stepmother remains in her bat-like shape, and a single glance at her little face will lead us to doubt whether she has repented of her evil deed.

Ozma and the Little Wizard

By L Frank Baum

ONCE UPON A TIME there lived in the beautiful Emerald City, which lies in the centre of the fair Land of Oz, a lovely girl called Princess Ozma, who was ruler of that country. Among those who served her was a little, withered old man known as the Wizard of Oz.

This little wizard could do a good many things in magic, but he was a kind man, so, instead of fearing him because of his magic, everybody loved him.

Ozma decided one morning to make a journey to all parts of the country, so that she might discover if there was any wrong that ought to be righted. She asked the little wizard to accompany her on her trip, and he was glad to go.

So the two left the Emerald City and wandered over the country for many days. Stopping one morning at a cottage, built beside the rocky path which led into a pretty valley beyond, Ozma asked a man, "Are you happy? Have you any complaint to make of your lot?"

And the man replied, "We are happy except for three mischievous imps that often come here to annoy us. If strangers pass through the valley the imps jeer at them, make horrid faces and often throw stones at them for no good reason."

They told the good man that they would see what could be done to protect him from the imps and at once entered the valley.

Before long they came upon three caves, hollowed from the rocks, and in front of each cave squatted a strange little dwarf. They had big round ears, flat noses and wide grinning mouths, and dark hair that came to points on top of their heads, much resembling horns. One of them suddenly reached out a hand and caught the dress of the princess, jerking it so that she nearly fell down, and another imp pushed the little wizard so hard that he bumped against Ozma and both unexpectedly sat down upon the ground.

At this the imps laughed boisterously and began running around in a circle, kicking dust upon the Royal Princess, who cried, "Wizard, do your duty!"

The wizard promptly obeyed. He opened his bag and muttered a spell.

Instantly the three Imps became three bushes — of a thorny stubby kind — with their roots in the ground.

"They can't help being good now, your Highness," said the wizard.

But something must have been wrong with the wizard's magic, or the creatures had magic of their own, for no sooner were the words spoken than the bushes began to move. Pretty soon they began to slide over the ground, their roots dragging through the earth. One pricked the wizard so sharply with its thorns that he cried out in pain.

Ozma sprang behind a tree and shouted, "Quick! Wizard, transform them into something else."

The wizard heard her, and grabbing from his bag the first magical tool he could find, he transformed the bushes into three pigs. That astonished the imps. In the shape of pigs — fat, roly-poly and cute — they scampered off a little distance and sat down to think about what to do next.

Ozma drew a long breath and coming from behind the tree she said, "That is much better, for pigs must be quite harmless."

But the imps were now angry and had no intention of behaving. As Ozma and the little wizard turned away from them, the

three pigs rushed forwards, dashed between their legs, and tripped them up, so that both lost their balance and toppled over.

As the wizard tried to get up he was tripped again and fell across the back of the third pig, which carried him on a run until it dumped the little man in the river. Ozma could not help laughing at his woeful appearance when he climbed out of the water and onto the riverbank.

The pigs tried to trip Princess Ozma, too, but she ran around a tree stump and managed to keep out of their way. So the wizard scrambled out of the water again and mumbled a magic mutter to dry his clothes, then he hurried off to help Ozma.

"This simply won't do," said the princess. "The pig imps would annoy travellers as much as the real imps. Please transform them into something else, Wiz."

So the wizard thought, then he changed the pigs into three blue doves.

"Doves," said he with a smile, "are the most harmless things in the world — the imps can't get up to mischief as birds."

But scarcely had he spoken when the doves flew at them and tried to peck out their eyes. When they shielded their eyes with their hands, two of the doves bit the wizard's fingers and another caught the pretty pink ear of the princess in its bill so that she cried out in pain.

"These birds are worse than pigs, Wizard," she called. "You must transform the imps into something that is not alive."

The wizard was pretty busy, just then, driving off the birds, but he managed to open his bag of magic and find a charm, which changed the doves into three buttons.

As they fell to the ground he picked them up and smiled. The wizard then placed the buttons in a little box, which he put in his jacket pocket to keep safe.

"Now," said he, "the imps cannot annoy travellers. We shall take them with us to the Emerald City."

"But we dare not use the buttons," said Ozma, smiling once more now that the danger was over.

"Why not?" asked the wizard. "I intend to sew them upon my coat and watch them carefully. The spirits of the imps are still in the buttons, and after a time they will be sorry for their naughtiness and may decide to be very good in the future. When they feel that way, I shall then restore them to their proper forms."

"Ah, that is magic well worthwhile," exclaimed Ozma, well pleased. "There is no doubt, my friend, but that you are a very clever wizard."

The Flower Princess

and other princess stories

Compiled by Tig Thomas

Miles
Kelly

First published in 2013 by Miles Kelly Publishing Ltd
Harding's Barn, Bardfield End Green, Thaxted, Essex, CM6 3PX, UK

This edition printed 2014

2 4 6 8 10 9 7 5 3

Publishing Director Belinda Gallagher
Creative Director Jo Cowan
Editorial Director Rosie Neave
Senior Editor Claire Philip
Senior Designer Joe Jones
Production Manager Elizabeth Collins
Reprographics Stephan Davis, Jennifer Cozens, Thom Allaway
Assets Lorraine King

ISBN 978-1-78209-211-7

Printed in China

British Library Cataloguing-in-Publication Data
A catalogue record for this book is available from the British Library

ACKNOWLEDGEMENTS

The publishers would like to thank the following artists who have contributed to this book:
Marcin Piwowarski, Kirsten Wilson, Mélanie Florian (inc. cover), Smiljana Coh

All other artwork from the Miles Kelly Artwork Bank

The publishers would like to thank the following sources for the use of their photographs:
Cover frame: Karina Bakalyan/Shutterstock.com
Inside frame: asmjp/Shutterstock.com

Made with paper from a sustainable forest

www.mileskelly.net   info@mileskelly.net

Contents

The Princess Emily

A retelling of **The Knight's Tale**
by Geoffrey Chaucer

MANY YEARS AGO, there lived a noble king called Theseus, with his wife Hippolyta, the queen of the Amazons, and her niece, Princess Emily. Emily was as lovely as a pure white lily upon its stalk of delicate green.

On the first day of May, she awoke early and went to gather flowers and sing about the joys of the morning. She had never looked more lovely, with her hands full of flower blossoms and the sun shining on her

beautiful blonde hair.

It just so happened that King Theseus had two knights in his prison. They had been captured fighting against him. Their names were Palamon and Arcite and they were best friends.

On this day, Palamon heard Emily singing and went to look out of the dark window from which he could catch a glimpse of the gardens. He gasped and cried, "A goddess!

Surely she must be a goddess! Maybe even Venus, the goddess of love herself." And in that moment Palamon's heart belonged to Emily forever.

Arcite leapt up and looked out of the window for himself.

"That's no goddess!" he cried, "but the most beautiful human the gods have ever made. I shall love her all my life."

"But Arcite," cried Palamon, "I saw her and fell in love with her first. Surely you will respect that?"

"You didn't even know she was a human," said Arcite. "I fell in love with a girl — you only worshipped a goddess."

In just one moment their friendship was finished forever. Each hoped to win Emily one day, and neither would speak to the other again. Their only joy came from watching Emily walk in the gardens whilst loving her from afar.

Many months later, Arcite's ransom was paid, and King Theseus released him back to his home country of Thebes. There he pined away dreaming only of the beautiful Emily. His face grew pale and his body lost its strength. Then he had an idea.

'No one would know me now,' he thought. 'I shall return to the court of King Theseus as a servant.'

This he did, becoming a squire of King Theseus. His joy was in spending time near Emily, bringing logs in for her fire, watching her dance, sing or talk but never daring to speak to her directly.

After seven long years in prison, Palamon finally escaped. He went to the forest, and one day while he was hiding there, Arcite came riding through on his horse. It was May Day once more, and he had come to gather a woodland garland for Emily's rooms. As he gathered green leaves, he sang a song in praise of his one true love. Suddenly Palamon leapt out of his hiding place and shouted fiercely. "Emily has only one true love and that is I, Palamon!"

The two men then flung themselves upon each other in a desperate rage. Palamon was like a raging lion and Arcite like a hungry tiger.

Heaven knows how the fight would have ended, but King Theseus came riding by with the queen, Princess Emily and his court. They found the two men now apart, out of breath.

"What's this? Who dares to fight in the royal forests?" King Theseus cried.

The two men were too angry to be careful, so they told the king their story.

"So you are Palamon and Arcite," said Theseus at last, "Palamon who has escaped from prison and Arcite who has unlawfully returned to my lands. I condemn you both to immediate death."

With tears in her eyes, Emily slipped off her horse and knelt in front of Theseus. "My Lord," she said, "I beg for the lives of these two young men. It is not their fault that they have been struck by cupid's arrow. I knew nothing of their love, but to kill them would be cruel."

The queen also pleaded with Theseus, and in the end he gave in. "Very well," he said to the two men. "Go back home, collect a hundred knights and return here. We will have a tournament, and the winner shall marry Princess Emily."

So Palamon and Arcite went away to call their friends together, and Emily sat in her high tower room, wondering which man she liked the best.

Theseus built a wonderful arena with stands, a jousting ring and three temples — one to Mars, the god of war, one to Venus, the goddess of love, and one to Diana, the goddess of young maidens.

Palamon and Arcite returned the night before the tournament, and each of them went to pray for success.

Arcite went to the temple of war. "Oh great god Mars," he prayed, "Give me victory in tomorrow's fight."

Palamon went to the temple of love. "Oh gentle goddess," he prayed, "let me win Princess Emily's heart."

Emily went to the temple of Diana. "If I am to marry, let it be to the one who will love me best."

The next day the tournament began. There was a great arranging of armour, fixing of spear-heads, buckling of helmets and polishing of shields. The trumpets sounded the charge. Out flew the swords, gleaming like polished silver. The fight was long and hard, but in the end Palamon was captured and Arcite was declared the winner. Full of excitement at his victory, he threw away his helmet and rode up the field to celebrate.

But the gods had planned so that all of the prayers might be answered. Arcite's horse stumbled and fell, throwing him heavily to the ground. He tragically died of his injuries, blessing Emily and begging Palamon's forgiveness with his last breath.

So Palamon won the fair Emily and long did they live in

bliss together. Emily loved Palamon tenderly, and he served her with so much gentleness that no word of anger was ever heard between them.

The Minstrel's Song

By Maud Lindsay

ONCE, LONG, LONG AGO, in a country over the sea there lived a prince called René, who married a lovely princess called Imogen.

Imogen came across the sea to the prince's beautiful country, and all his people welcomed her with great joy because the prince loved her.

"What can I do to please you today?"

the prince asked her every morning. One day the princess answered that she would like to hear all the minstrels in the prince's country, for they were said to be the finest in the world.

As soon as the prince heard this, he called his heralds and sent them throughout his land to sound their trumpets and call aloud, "Hear you minstrels! Prince René bids you come to play at his court on May Day, for love of the princess."

The minstrels were men who sang beautiful songs and played harps, and long ago they went about from place to place, from castle to castle, from palace to palace, and were always sure of a welcome wherever they roamed.

They could sing of the brave deeds of knights, and of wars and battles, and could tell of the mighty hunters who hunted in the great forests, and of fairies and goblins, better than a storybook. And because there were no storybooks in those days, everybody was glad to see them come.

So when the minstrels heard the prince's message, they hurried to the palace on May Day, and it so happened that some of them met on the way and decided to travel along together.

One of these minstrels was a young man named Harmonius. While the others talked of the songs they would sing, he gathered wildflowers from the roadside.

"I can sing of the drums and battles," said the oldest minstrel, whose hair was white and whose step was slow.

"I can sing of ladies and their fair faces," said the youngest minstrel, but Harmonius whispered, "Stop and listen! Listen!"

"We hear nothing at all but the wind in the tree-tops," said the others. "We have no time to stop."

They hurried on and left Harmonius. He stood under the trees and listened, for he heard something very sweet. At last he realized that it was the wind singing of its travels through the world, telling how it raced over the sea, tossing the waves and rocking the ships, and hurried on to the hills, where the trees made harps of their branches, and then how it blew down into the valleys, where all the flowers danced in time.

Harmonius listened until he

17

knew the whole song, and then he ran on to reach his friends, who were still talking of the incredible sights that they were to about to see.

"We shall see the prince and speak to him," said the oldest minstrel.

"And his golden crown and the princess's jewels," added the youngest. Harmonius had no chance to tell of the wind's song.

Now their path led them through the wood. As they talked, Harmonius said, "Hush! Listen!" But the others said, "Oh! That is only the sound of the brook trickling over the stones. Let us make haste to the prince's court."

But Harmonius stayed to hear the joyful song that the brook was singing, of its journey through mosses and ferns and shady ways, and of tumbling over the rocks in shining waterfalls on its long journey to the sea.

Harmonius sat and listened until he knew every word of the song off by heart, and then he hurried on to catch up with the others.

When he reached the others once more, they were still talking of the prince and princess, so he could not tell them of the brook. Then he heard something once again that was wonderfully sweet, and he cried, "Listen! Listen!"

"Oh! That is only a bird!" the others replied. "Let us make haste to the court, it is not far now."

But Harmonius would not go. The bird sang so joyfully that

The Minstrel's Song

Harmonius laughed when he heard its song. The bird was singing a song of green trees, and in every tree a nest, and in every nest some eggs! "Thank you, little bird," he said, "you have taught me a song." And he made haste to join his friends, for the palace was near.

When they arrived they were taken to see the prince and princess. The prince was thinking of the princess and the minstrels, but the princess was imagining her old home, and of the butterflies she had chased when she was a little child. One by one the minstrels played their harps before them. The oldest minstrel sang of battles and drums. The youngest minstrel sang of ladies and their fair faces, which pleased the court ladies very much.

Then came Harmonius. When he touched his harp and sang, the song sounded like the wind blowing, the sea roaring and the trees creaking. Then it grew very soft, and sounded like a trickling brook dripping on stones and running over little pebbles, and while the prince and princess and all the court listened in surprise, Harmonius's song grew ever sweeter. The princess shut her eyes as she listened to the music.

Then the prince came down from his throne to ask Harmonius if he came from fairyland with such a wonderful song. But Harmonius answered, "Three singers sang along the way, and I learnt the song from them today."

All the other minstrels looked up in

surprise when Harmonius spoke, and the oldest minstrel said, "We heard no music on our way."

But the princess said, "That is an old song. I heard it when I was a little child, and I can name the three singers." And so she did. Can you name them too?

How Prin Angelica Took a Little Maid

An extract from **The Rose and the Ring**
by William Makepeace Thackeray

One day, when Princess Angelica was still quite a little girl, she was walking in the garden of the palace with Mrs Gruffanuff, the governess. She was on her way to the royal pond to see the swans and ducks, and was carrying a bun to feed them.

Angelica had not yet reached the duck pond, when a funny little girl came toddling up. She had a great quantity of hair blowing about her chubby little cheeks, and she looked as if she had not been washed for a long while.

The little girl wore a ragged bit of a cloak, and only one shoe.

"You little wretch, who on earth let you in here?" asked Mrs Gruffanuff angrily.

"Can I have dat bun?"

said the little girl, "me vely hungy."

"Hungry! What is that?" asked Princess Angelica, and she gave the child the bun.

"Oh, Princess!" said Mrs Gruffanuff, "How good, how truly angelical you are! See, Your Majesties," she said to the king and queen, who now came walking up to them, "how kind the princess is! She met this little wretch in the garden — I can't tell you why the guards did not stop her at the gate — and the dear princess has given her the whole of her bun!"

"But Mrs Gruffanuff, I didn't want it," said Angelica.

"You are a darling little angel all the same," said the governess.

"Yes, I know I am," said Angelica. "Dirty little girl, don't you think I am very pretty?"

Indeed, the princess had on the finest of little dresses, and, as her hair was carefully curled, she looked very pretty indeed.

"Oh, pooty, pooty!" said the little girl, laughing, dancing and munching her bun. As she ate it she began to sing, "Oh, what fun to have a plum bun! How I wis it never was done!" At which they all began to laugh merrily.

"I can dance as well as sing," said the little girl. "I can dance, and I can sing, and I can do all sorts of ting."

And she ran to a flowerbed, pulled out some flowers, made herself a little wreath, and danced before the king and queen so comically and prettily, that everybody was delighted.

"Who was your mother — who were your relations, little girl?" said the queen.

The little girl said, "Little lion was my brudder, great big lioness my mudder, neber heard of any udder."

So Angelica said to the queen, "My parrot flew away out of its cage yesterday, and I no longer care for any of my toys. I think this little dirty child will amuse me. I will take her home, and give her my old frocks…"

"Oh, the generous darling!" said Mrs Gruffanuff.

"…which I have worn ever so many times, and am quite tired of," Angelica went on, "and she shall be my maid. Will you come home with me, little girl?"

The child clapped her hands, and said, "Go home with you — yes!"

And they all laughed again, and took the child to the palace. The girl was given a

bath, and once washed and
combed she looked as
pretty as Angelica,

almost. Not that Angelica ever thought so,
for this little lady never imagined that
anybody in the world could be as pretty, as

good or as clever as her fine self.

In order that the little girl should not become too proud, Mrs Gruffanuff took her old ragged cloak and one shoe, and put them into a glass box. A card was then laid upon them, upon which was written,

These were the old clothes in which little Betsinda was found when the great goodness and admirable kindness of Her Royal Highness the Princess Angelica received this little outcast.

And the date was added, and the box locked up.

For a while little Betsinda was a great

favourite with the princess. She danced, sang, and made little rhymes to amuse her mistress. But then the princess got a monkey, and afterwards a little dog. After that she got a doll, and did not care for Betsinda any more. Betsinda became very quiet and sang no more funny songs, because nobody cared to hear her.

And then, as she grew older, she was made a little lady's maid to the princess, and though she had no wages, she worked hard and mended, and put Angelica's hair in papers, and was never cross when scolded, and was always eager to please. She was always up early and to bed late, and at hand when wanted, and in fact became a perfect little maid.

So the two girls grew up, and Betsinda was never tired of waiting on the princess.

She made her dresses better than the best
dress-maker, and was useful in many ways.

Whilst the princess was having her
lessons, Betsinda would watch, and in this
way she picked up a great deal of learning
– for she was always awake, though her
mistress was not, and listened to
the wise professors when Angelica
was snoozing or
thinking of the
next ball.

And when the dancing-master came, Betsinda learned along with Angelica, and when the music-master came, she watched him and practised the princess's pieces when Angelica was away at balls and parties. When the drawing-master came she took note of all he said and did — and the same with French, Italian and all the other languages.

When the princess was going out in the evening she would say, "Betsinda, you may as well finish what I have begun."

"Yes, miss," Betsinda would say, and sit down very cheerfully, not to FINISH what Angelica began, but to DO it.

For instance, the princess would begin to draw, let us say, a head of a warrior, but Betsinda would finish it. The princess would put her name to the drawing, and the court and king and queen would admire it, saying, "Was there ever a genius like Angelica?"

So, I am sorry to say, was it with the princess's embroidery and other accomplishments. Angelica actually believed that she did these things herself, and received all the flattery of the court as if every word of it was true. Thus she began to think that there was no young woman in all the world equal to herself, and that no young man was good enough for her. She had a very high opinion of herself indeed.

As for Betsinda, she heard none of these praises, so she was not puffed up by them, and being a most grateful, good-natured girl, she was only too anxious to do everything that might please her mistress.

So now you begin to perceive that

Angelica had faults of her own, and was by no means such a wonder of wonders as many people represented Her Royal Highness to be.

The Flower Princess

Anon

THERE WAS ONCE a princess so fair and lovely that the sun shone more brightly on her than on anyone else, the river stopped running when she walked by so that it might gaze on her beauty, and birds sang underneath her window at night.

Princes came to beg for her hand in marriage, but she swore she would only marry a prince who was kind, good and true. Many princes tried to convince her of their fine qualities, but none succeeded — until one day a prince from a small

The Flower Princess

kingdom came to woo her. He fell in love with her, she could not resist him, and they were married. She wore a silver dress embroidered with crystal drops and looked lovely. The court scattered her path with rose petals and threw sugar sweets as the couple walked past.

But alas, trouble can come to all of us.

The prince's kingdom had an evil fairy. She was very beautiful but her beauty was spoilt by the cruelty and mean thoughts that she held inside.

When she saw the princess with her sweet, good face, her heart filled with jealousy and rage. She wove a spell to transform the princess into a flower in a nearby meadow.

The spell was not quite powerful enough to conquer the princess completely, so by night she appeared again in her true form, but every morning she had to transform into her flowery shape and spend the day in the meadow standing among the grasses and the other flowers.

One night she overheard the fairy talking and learnt how to break the spell. She told her husband, "If you come to the meadow

The Flower Princess

in the morning and pick me the
spell will be broken."
"How will I know
which one is you?" he said.
The princess did not know, for
her shape changed every day.
That morning she changed into a flower
and the prince hastened to the field to try
and find his love. He walked among the
grasses and the many flowers. How could
he find his love?
Then a thought came to him and he
looked closely at each bloom. Finally he
stopped before a blue cornflower, touched it
gently with his fingers, plucked it and
carried it back to his palace. As he passed
through the gates, the flower fell to the
ground and his princess stood before him.
"How did you find me?" she asked.

"Dew had fallen on all of the other flowers," he replied, "you alone had no dew upon you, for you had spent the night at the palace."

Hans Christian Andersen

The Princess and the Pea

and other fairy tales

Miles
Kelly

First published in 2015 by Miles Kelly Publishing Ltd
Harding's Barn, Bardfield End Green, Thaxted, Essex, CM6 3PX, UK

2 4 6 8 10 9 7 5 3 1

Publishing Director Belinda Gallagher
Creative Director Jo Cowan
Editorial Director Rosie Neave
Editor Amy Johnson
Designers Rob Hale, Joe Jones
Production Manager Elizabeth Collins
Reprographics Stephan Davis, Jennifer Cozens, Thom Allaway

ISBN 978-1-78209-773-0

Printed in China

British Library Cataloguing-in-Publication Data
A catalogue record for this book is available from the British Library

ACKNOWLEDGEMENTS
The publishers would like to thank the following artists who have contributed to this book:

Front cover: Rosie Butcher (The Bright Agency)

Inside illustrations:
The Princess and the Pea Claudia Venturini (Plum Pudding Illustration Agency)
The Tinder Box Martina Peluso (Advocate-art)
The Flying Trunk Christine Battuz (Advocate-art)
The Buckwheat Kristina Swarner (The Bright Agency)

Border illustrations: Louise Ellis (The Bright Agency)

Made with paper from a sustainable forest

www.mileskelly.net
info@mileskelly.net

Contents

The Princess and the Pea

Once upon a time there was a prince who wanted to marry a princess – but she had to be a *real* princess.

So he set off to find one. The prince journeyed all over the world, visiting countries near and far, and he met many princesses on his travels. But not one of them would do. Out of all the hundreds of pretty (and plain), clever (and foolish), entertaining (and boring), good-hearted (and mean-natured) princesses that the prince met, he didn't think any of them had that special something that made them a real princess.

After years of searching, the prince finally gave up hope. He headed home again, his heart filled with great sadness, for he wished so much to have a real princess to love.

One evening, the prince was sitting with his father and mother by the fire in his castle, while a terrible storm raged outside. Towering black clouds blotted out the stars.

Howling gusts of wind tore at the castle turrets. Torrents of rain came crashing onto the battlements. Daggers of lightning slashed through the sky and ear-splitting thunder exploded overhead. It was truly terrifying!

Suddenly, in the midst of the din, the prince heard a steady banging. Whatever could it be? It sounded very much like someone knocking at the castle door, but who would brave being outside in such terrible weather?

The prince and his parents listened carefully… Yes, there it was again – it was definitely someone knocking at the castle door. Very puzzled – and a little worried – the old king went to answer it.

To his great amazement, a young woman was standing there. And good gracious, what a sight she looked! The wind had wound her hair into tangles and the rain had soaked her through – she looked as though she had been tumbled about in a whirlpool and then forced to stand under a waterfall.

As the old king ushered the bedraggled girl inside, the water ran from her hair and clothes, and from the end of her nose. The old queen arrived in the hall to find her shivering with drips trickling into the toes of her shoes and running out again at the heels.

And yet, even though the girl didn't look royal, she insisted that she was a princess.

'Hmm,' thought the old queen, raising an eyebrow. 'We'll soon find that out.' But she said nothing at all. Instead, she hurried off to the finest guest room and stripped all the bedding off the bed – she even heaved the huge mattress off as well.

Then she placed a single pea, very carefully, on top of the bare bed frame, right in the middle. Finally, she replaced the mattress and called for servants to layer another nineteen mattresses on top – the thickest that could be found – and then pile twenty duckfeather quilts on top of that.

Meanwhile, the princess had been given towels and hot soup and was recovering by the fire. When the old queen was satisfied that everything was ready, the princess was shown to the guest room. She didn't bat an eyelid at the mountainous bed that stood before her. She just said a very heartfelt thank you and shut the door.

The next morning, the first thing the old queen said to the princess was to enquire politely if she had slept well enough.

"Oh dreadfully, I am afraid," sighed the princess. "I have hardly closed my eyes all night. Heaven only knows what was in my bed, but I was lying on something hard. I am bruised black and blue all over!"

Then the royal family knew that the girl truly was a real princess, for she had felt the tiny pea through the twenty mattresses and twenty quilts. Only a *real* princess could possibly be that sensitive.

The prince was overjoyed – he had found the right girl at last! The couple were soon married, and indeed lived happily ever after.

As for the pea, well, it was put on display in a museum, where you can still see it today (if no one has stolen it by now).

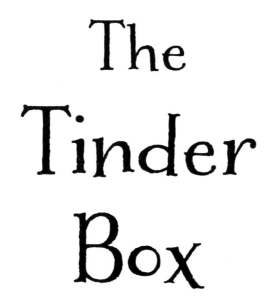

The Tinder Box

Asoldier was on his way home from war when he met an old witch who said, "You look very brave! I am sure you deserve lots of money – and I know of a way you can get it. See that large tree with the hole in its trunk? It is hollow inside. Tie a rope around the trunk and let it tumble inside. Then climb through the hole.

"You will find yourself in a hall with three doors. Go into the first room and there will be a chest on the floor. On the chest will be a dog, with eyes as large as teacups. Don't be afraid. I will give you my blue checked apron – spread it on the floor, then put the dog on it and he won't hurt you. The chest will be full of copper coins – you can take them all.

"However, if you would rather have silver, go into the second room. Here you will find another chest with a dog on it that has eyes as big as mill-wheels. Put the dog on my apron, open the chest and take the silver.

"But if you like gold best, go into the third room. There will be a dog there whose eyes are as big as castle turrets. Take him off the chest and put him on my apron. Then you can take as much gold as you like.

"In return, all I want is a tinder box that's in there," said the witch. "You know – the sort of box that people keep bits of flint in, for sparking up a fire."

"Very well," said the soldier.

So the witch gave him her blue checked apron and the soldier went inside the tree.

Everything was just as the witch had said. The first dog was terrifying! But he followed the witch's instructions and the dog didn't hurt him. The soldier filled his pockets and knapsack with copper. But in the second room, he threw away the copper coins and filled his pockets and knapsack with silver instead. In the third room, he threw away the silver and filled his pockets, knapsack, cap and boots with gold! Then he found the tinder

box and clambered back out of the tree.

"Give me the tinder box," said the witch.

"Tell me why you want it," said the soldier cleverly, "or I will cut off your head."

The witch turned red with fury. "No," she said, and began to mutter a magic spell.

At once, the soldier drew his sword and cut off her head. Then he went to the nearest town, where he stayed at the best inn – for now he had plenty of money. Everyone saw that the soldier was rich and wanted to get to know him. And as he talked to people, he came to hear of the king's beautiful daughter.

"No one is allowed to see her," one of his new friends explained. "A wise woman once told the king that the princess would marry a

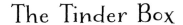

common soldier. The king was so horrified that he shut the princess away in the castle."

'I would like very much to see the princess,' thought the soldier. Then he remembered the witch's tinder box. He waited till midnight, then took a piece of flint out of the tinder box and struck it.

The dog with eyes as big as teacups appeared. "What are your orders, O master?"

"Er… I would like to see the princess," said the astonished soldier.

The dog disappeared and returned in a flash, with the sleeping princess on his back. She looked so lovely that the soldier could not help kissing her, before the dog took her back.

In the morning, the princess told the king

and queen that she had had a very strange dream. A dog had taken her to a soldier, who had kissed her! Next night, the queen set her oldest lady-in-waiting to keep watch.

The soldier longed to see the princess once more, so he struck the flint again, and the dog with eyes as big as teacups appeared as before. When ordered, the dog fetched the princess. But the lady-in-waiting followed and marked the door of the soldier's inn with a chalk cross. She went home and the dog presently returned the princess. But when the dog saw the cross, he put one on every other door too!

The next night, the queen filled a little bag with buckwheat flour, and cut a tiny hole in it. She then tied it round the princess's neck.

During the night, the dog
with eyes like teacups came and
carried off the princess to the soldier – who
had fallen deeply in love with her. But the
dog did not notice the flour running out of
the bag all the way to the soldier's window.
So in the morning, the king and queen found
out where their daughter had been, and the
soldier was put in prison.

In his cell, the soldier stood on tiptoe and
peeped out through the little barred window.

He called to a passing shoemaker's boy: "Run to the best inn in town and fetch my tinder box, and I will give you five gold coins."

So the shoemaker's boy did, double-quick.

Then the soldier struck the flint in the tinder box one… two… three times – and there stood all the dogs: the one with eyes as big as teacups, the one with eyes as large as mill-wheels, and the third, whose eyes were like castle turrets. They leapt together at the prison wall and burst through it as if it were paper. The soldier was free! When all the townspeople saw him appear with his magical servants, they clapped and cheered.

"Hooray!" they cried. "What a hero! You should marry the beautiful princess!"

The king and queen were forced to agree – otherwise the people would have rioted. So the soldier married the beautiful princess and became a prince. Everyone celebrated joyfully, while the dogs were guests of honour at the wedding feast and sat staring with their massive eyes.

The Flying Trunk

Long ago and far away, there was a merchant who was so rich that he could have paved the whole town with gold – and still have bags more left over. Of course, he wasn't silly enough to do such a thing. In fact, he used his money very wisely, so he made bags more. By the time the merchant died, he was an enormously wealthy man. All his heaps of money passed to his son – who wasted it quicker than you could say 'down the drainpipe.'

He used notes to make paper aeroplanes, and skimmed gold coins into the sea – and very soon the fortune was all gone. Then he found his friends were gone too – for they were all nasty people who had only liked him because he was rich. In fact, one of them sent him an old trunk with a message: Pack up!

"Yes, pack up," the young man said, "that would be a good idea, if I had anything left to pack!" So he just climbed into the trunk himself and sat, fiddling with the lock.

To his great amazement, as he pressed on it, away flew the trunk right up into the clouds! Off he soared, all the way to the land of Turkey. Then he pressed the lock once more and the trunk came gently down to earth.

The young man was delighted with the magic trunk, which had cheered him up a great deal. He hid it carefully in a wood,

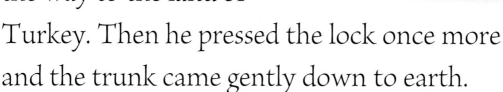

covering it with branches and leaves, and then made his way to a nearby town. He wandered around, exploring, until he came to a magnificent castle. He asked a passerby who lived there. "The king's daughter," the woman replied. "She is very beautiful."

"Thank you," said the young man. He walked around for a while longer, thinking about the princess. He decided he wanted to meet her, and so he hurried back to the trunk, and flew it up to the roof of the castle. He landed there, then crept through a window into the princess's bedroom.

She lay there, asleep, and she was so beautiful that he couldn't take his eyes off her. As he stood there, the princess woke up and was very frightened. So the young man told her a fib – he said he was an angel, who had come down from heaven to see her.

The princess was delighted at this. The young man entertained her by telling stories, and she found him very charming.

When he asked her to marry him, she said yes at once. "But you must come on Saturday," she said, "for then my father and mother are coming to tea. They will be very pleased when they hear I am going to marry an angel. Make sure you think of some more wonderful stories, for my parents like to hear stories better than anything. My mother likes tales that teach a lesson, but my father likes funny stories that make him laugh."

"Very well," the young man replied, and said goodbye. But before he went, the princess gave him a gift – a sword studded with gold coins.

The young man then flew straight to the town, where he exchanged the sword for some fine new clothes which would be fit for meeting the king and queen. Then he went back to the wood where he could sit alone and think, and make up a story for Saturday.

When the day finally came, he flew back to the castle. There, the princess, king, queen – and in fact the whole court – were waiting for the angel. They welcomed him most politely, and then the queen said: "Will you tell us a story that teaches us something?"

"But one that makes us laugh too," added the king.

"Certainly," he replied, and so he began. "My story is called 'The Last Laugh'. There was once a princess who met a man who said he was an angel. He then made the king and queen believe that he was an angel too."

The king began to chuckle. "What a silly family," he said. "How could they fall for something like that?"

The young man continued, "So when the angel asked for the princess's hand in marriage, the answer was yes. After the wedding, the princess and her parents found out that the man didn't have wings and wasn't an angel after all. But in fact, he could

actually fly. For he had a magic trunk which he could sit in and soar through the air. So the man had the last laugh, for they thought he was as good as an angel after all.

"And the moral of this story is: never believe what people tell you, unless you have seen proof."

Then the queen clapped her hands and the king shouted "Bravo!" and the courtiers all murmured to each other in delight.

Only the princess sat in silence, thinking.

Still, the wedding day was fixed for later that week. The evening before, a great festival was held in the town so everyone could celebrate. The king ordered that cakes were to be given out among the people, and bands played music outdoors so everyone could dance in the streets. Jugglers and acrobats performed among the crowds, and everyone thought it was a very jolly affair.

'I will give them another treat,' thought the merchant's son. So he went and bought rockets and Catherine wheels and every sort of firework that you can think of. He packed them in his trunk and flew up into the air.

What a whizzing and popping they made as they burst open like flowers! And how amazed everyone was to see him in the sky!

But alas, a spark from one of the fireworks landed on the trunk and set it alight. The merchant's son only just made it back down to the ground before the smouldering object

burst into flames and burned away to ashes.

So the merchant's son could not fly any more, nor go to meet his bride. But perhaps that was just as well. She had realized that she had been tricked and was waiting to kick him out of the kingdom, for of course she didn't want to marry a liar – flying trunk or no flying trunk.

Today, the merchant's son wanders through the world making a living by telling fairy tales, but none of them are as entertaining as his own story.

The Buckwheat

From its name, buckwheat sounds as if it should be a cereal, like wheat or rye. But it is not a grain. It is not even a grass. It is in fact a flowering wild plant with seeds that can be used in cooking or ground down to make flour.

If you come across a field of buckwheat after there has been a violent thunderstorm, very often it looks blackened and burned, as if it has been briefly set on fire. People who live in the countryside say

33

that it gets singed in the lightning. But sparrows say that the lightning strikes it down on purpose.

The sparrows told me once that they heard the real reason why from a willow tree. He is a very old and distinguished willow tree, and completely to be trusted – even if he does look rather crippled by age. His trunk has split and brambles and grass have taken root there. The tree stoops forward slightly and the branches hang quite down to the ground,

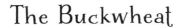

just like wispy strands of green hair.

Today in the surrounding fields different types of corn grow there – not only rye and barley but also oats. The oats are the prettiest; when the grains are ripe they look like little golden canary-birds sitting on a bough. But all the corn looks beautiful, standing in the sunshine. When the ears are heavy with grain they bend and nod humbly.

Once, long ago, a field of buckwheat grew there too, exactly opposite the old willow tree. But the buckwheat did not bend like the grain. Instead, it stood up straight and stiff, holding its head up proudly.

"I am just as important as all the corn," one of the buckwheat plants remarked boastfully to the willow tree one day, "and I must say, I am *much* more beautiful! My flowers are as pretty as apple blossom. It's quite a delight to look at me and my family. You must agree, old willow tree. Do you know of any plant prettier than we are?"

At that moment a breeze blew around the willow tree. He nodded his head and dipped his branches as if to say, 'Indeed I do.'

The buckwheat wasn't put off at all. In fact, the plant spread herself out even wider with pride. "Stupid tree!" she scoffed rudely. "He's so old and has been there so long that he's got grass sprouting out of his body!"

Time went by and one night, a terrible storm blew up. The wind howled and

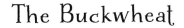

plucked at the plants with strong fingers. The rain lashed down on them. All the plants in the cornfields hurried to fold up their leaves and bow their heads, to try to avoid harm. But the buckwheat plants refused to do so. They simply stood up straighter than ever.

"Bow down as we do," urged the other wildflowers, worriedly.

"Why should we?" replied the buckwheat.

"Bow down as we do," cried the ears of corn. "The angel of the storm is coming, and his wings spread from the sky above to the earth down below. He will cut you in half before you can even cry out."

"There's nothing that can make us bow down," stated the buckwheat brazenly. "We will not bow down to anything."

"Lovely buckwheat, please close your leaves and lower your flowers," begged the old willow tree. "And whatever you do, do not look at the lightning when it strikes. When the skies split open it gives us a little glimpse into heaven – but it is so dazzling that even humans shouldn't gaze at it. It blinds them, so whatever would it do to us lesser beings?"

"Lesser beings, indeed!" snorted the buckwheat.

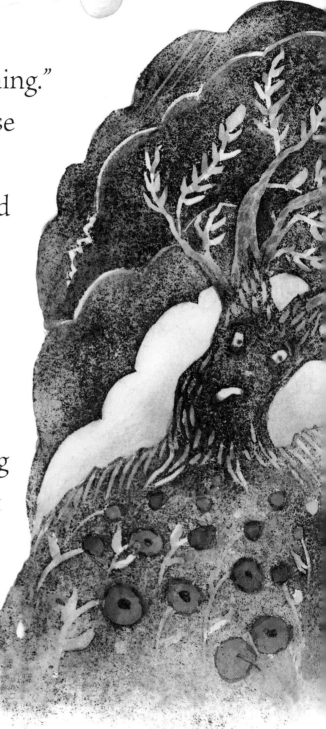

"Of course we're good enough to look into heaven!" And boldly all the buckwheat looked straight up, while the lightning blazed across the sky as if the whole world were in flames.

When the terrifying storm had died away, the wildflowers and the corn gently raised their drooping heads. The air was still and pure to breathe, and they felt quite refreshed by the rain. However, the buckwheat was a sorry sight. The plants were scorched black by the lightning and lay limply across the earth.

The old willow tree waved its branches in the wind and large drops of water fell from his green leaves, just as if he were weeping.

"Why do you cry," asked the sparrows, "when everything else is cheerful? Look, the sun is smiling and the clouds are floating in the blue. Can't you smell the scent of growing things? Tell us why you are weeping."

Then the willow told the sparrows why the buckwheat had met its sad end – that the lightning had punished it for its pride.

And this is the tale that the sparrows told me, in turn, when I asked them for a story…

The Frog Princess

and other princess stories

Compiled by Tig Thomas

Miles
KeLLY

First published in 2013 by Miles Kelly Publishing Ltd
Harding's Barn, Bardfield End Green, Thaxted, Essex, CM6 3PX, UK

This edition printed 2014

2 4 6 8 10 9 7 5 3

Publishing Director Belinda Gallagher
Creative Director Jo Cowan
Editorial Director Rosie Neave
Senior Editor Claire Philip
Senior Designer Joe Jones
Production Manager Elizabeth Collins
Reprographics Stephan Davis, Jennifer Cozens, Thom Allaway
Assets Lorraine King

ISBN 978-1-78209-220-9

Printed in China

British Library Cataloguing-in-Publication Data
A catalogue record for this book is available from the British Library

ACKNOWLEDGEMENTS
The publishers would like to thank the following artists who have contributed to this book:
Jennie Poh, Smiljana Coh, Mélanie Florian, Marcin Piwowarski, Helen Rowe (cover)

All other artwork from the Miles Kelly Artwork Bank

The publishers would like to thank the following sources for the use of their photographs:
Cover frame: Karina Bakalyan/Shutterstock.com
Inside frame: asmjp/Shutterstock.com

Made with paper from a sustainable forest
www.mileskelly.net   info@mileskelly.net

Contents

The Magic Key

By Howard Pyle

ONCE THERE WAS A PRINCE called John. One day his father said to him, "John, I am growing old, and I would very much like to see you married."

"Very well," said the prince, "and who shall I marry?"

"Why not the Princess of the White Mountain?" said the old king.

"Why not, indeed?" said the young prince, "only she is too short."

"Why not the Princess of the Blue Mountain?" said the old king.

"Why not, indeed?" said the young prince, "only she is too tall."

"Why not the Princess of the Red Mountain?" said the old king.

"Why not, indeed?" said the young prince, "only she is too pale."

"Then who will you marry?" said the old king in desperation.

"I do not know," said the young prince, "but her skin shall be as white as milk, her cheeks shall be as red as blood, her eyes shall be as blue as the skies, and her hair shall be like spun gold."

"Then go and find her!" said the king.

So the prince travelled on until his shoes were dusty and his clothes were grey.

Nothing was in his bag but a piece of brown bread and some cold meat. After a while he came to a crossroads, and there sat an old woman. She looked very sad.

"Please help me Sir, I am very hungry!" said the old woman.

The prince was a good-hearted fellow, so he said, "I only have a little food, but you are welcome to it." The old woman ate the prince's food as soon as he handed it to her.

"I am also very cold," said she.

"I only have this dusty coat, but you are welcome to it," said the prince.

"Thank you for your kindness," said the old woman, and she gave him an old rusty key. "If you look through the ring of it, you can see everything as it really is."

The prince wasn't sure what the old lady meant, but he travelled on, and at last he came to a castle that stood in the middle of a dark forest.

"I hope I shall find some food to

eat," said the prince, and he walked up the long path to the castle door, which he opened and went in. Only one person was within, and

that person was
a maiden. She
was covered in
black soot from
head to foot like
a charcoal burner
and dressed in
filthy rags. The
prince drew the rusty
key out of his pocket
and took a peep at
her through its ring.

He saw that she
was no longer
dirty, but as
beautiful as a
ripe apple – for
her skin was
as white as

milk, her cheeks were as red as blood, her eyes were as blue as the skies, and her hair was like spun gold.

"You are the one whom I seek," he said.

"Yes, I am," said she.

"And how can I free you from your enchantment?" the prince said.

"If you stay here three nights, and bear all that shall happen to you without a word, then I shall be free," said she.

"Oh yes, I will do that," said the prince. He had fallen in love at first sight.

After that the dirty princess set a supper before him, and the prince ate like a king.

A little while later there was a loud noise, the door opened, and in came an ugly troll with a head as big as a bucket. It rolled its great saucer eyes around till it saw the prince beside the fire.

"Black cats and spotted toads!" bellowed the troll. "Why are you here?"

But the prince never said a word.

The troll caught the prince by the hair and threw him around the room, but the prince never said a word. After a while the troll gave up and left.

The dirty princess found the prince tending his wounds and began to cry. When her tears fell on him his pain left him, and he was well again.

The next night the troll returned, and with him came two others. "Black cats and spotted toads!" bellowed the troll. "Are you here again?"

This time all three trolls flung the prince about, but he stayed quiet the whole time.

On the third night, the troll brought six others. The same thing happened as before, and they tried their best to make the prince make a sound. The poor prince was left very bruised, but he didn't say a word. He had fulfilled his task.

So, one last time, the princess came and wept over him, and before he knew it he was whole and sound again. The princess stood before him. Her skin was as white as milk, her cheeks were as red as blood, her eyes were as blue as the skies, and her hair was like spun gold.

Then the prince started his journey home, taking her with him. When they neared the palace the prince told the princess to wait for him nearby. He went and fetched her a dress of real silver and gold, such as was fitting for her to wear.

Then the happy couple rode into the town together where they were welcomed by all

The Magic Key

the people. The king was delighted that his son had found a bride at last and immediately ordered a grand wedding. The prince and the princess were overjoyed, and lived happily ever after for the rest of their days.

The Frog Princess

A traditional Russian tale

THERE WAS ONCE A KING who said to his three sons, "Let each of you shoot an arrow. The maiden who brings it back will be your bride." The eldest shot an arrow and a princess brought it back. The middle son let loose an arrow and a general's daughter brought it back. But Prince Ivan's arrow fell into a marsh and was brought back by a frog. The first two brothers were joyful but Prince Ivan was downcast. He wept, but there was nothing for it, he had to marry the frog. All three couples were married on the same day — the frog being held up on a silver tray.

Some time passed. One day the king wished to see which bride was the best at sewing. So he ordered them to make him a shirt. Poor Prince Ivan cried, "How can my frog sew a shirt? I'll be a laughing stock." The frog jumped across the floor croaking.

As soon as Prince Ivan was asleep the frog went outside, cast off her skin and turned into a beautiful maiden, calling, "Maids and matrons, sew me a shirt!" A host of servants appeared and brought a finely embroidered shirt. She took it and placed it beside Prince Ivan. Then she turned back into a frog as if nothing had happened.

In the morning Prince Ivan awoke and was overjoyed to find the shirt, which he took to the king. The king gazed at it and said, "Now there's a shirt for you, fit to wear on feast days!"

Then the middle brother brought a shirt, at which the king said, "This shirt is fit only for a cottage!" And taking the eldest brother's shirt, he said, "And this one is fit only for a smoky peasant hut!"

The king's sons went their separate ways, with the two eldest muttering among themselves, "We were surely wrong to mock at Prince Ivan's wife, she must be a cunning sorceress, not a frog."

Presently the king again issued another command. This time the two eldest son's wives were each to bake a loaf of bread, and bring it to him to judge which bride was the best cook. The other two brides had made fun of the frog, but now they sent a maid to see how she would bake her loaf. The frog noticed the woman, so she kneaded some dough, rolled it out and tipped it straight into the fire. The chambermaid ran to tell her mistresses, the royal brides, and they did the same.

But the crafty frog had tricked them. As soon as the woman had gone, she got the dough out, cast off her skin and called, "Maids and matrons, bake me a loaf of bread such as my dear father used to eat on Sundays and holidays." In an instant the maids and matrons brought the bread. She took it, placed it beside Prince Ivan, and turned into a frog again.

In the morning Prince Ivan awoke, took the loaf of bread and gave it to his father who looked at it and said, "Now this is bread fit to grace a holy day. It is not at all like the burnt offerings of my elder daughters-in-law!"

After that the king decided to hold a ball

to see which of his sons' wives was the best dancer. All the guests and daughters-in-law assembled. Everyone was there except Prince Ivan, who thought, 'How can I go to the ball with a frog?' The poor prince was very sad indeed. "Do not despair, Prince Ivan," said the frog. "Go to the ball. I shall follow in an hour." Prince Ivan was cheered at the frog's words, and left for the ball.

Then the frog cast off her skin and turned into a lovely maid dressed in finery. When she arrived at the ball, Prince

Ivan was overjoyed, and the guests clapped their hands at the sight of such beauty. When the ball was over, Prince Ivan rode off ahead of his wife, found the frogskin and burnt it. So when his wife returned and looked for the skin, it was nowhere to be seen. She said to her husband, "Oh, Prince Ivan, if only you had waited a little longer the spell I am under would have been broken and I, Yelena the Fair, would have been yours forever. Now God alone knows when we shall meet again. Farewell. If you wish to find me you must go beyond the Thrice-Nine Land to the Thrice-Ten Kingdom." And she vanished.

Prince Ivan set off to seek his princess. He came to a little hut, and cried, "Little hut turn your face to me, please, and your back to the trees." The little hut did as he said and Prince Ivan entered. There before him sat an old woman, who cried, "Fie, Foh! Where are you going, Prince Ivan?"

"I seek Yelena the Fair," he replied.

"Prince Ivan," the old woman said, "you've waited too long! She has begun to forget you and is to marry another. She is with my sister who will not wish her to return to you. Go there now, but beware — as you approach they will know it is you. Yelena will turn into a spindle, her dress will turn to gold. My sister will wind the gold thread around the spindle and put it into a box, which she will lock. You must find the key, open the box, and break the spindle. Then she will appear."

Off went Prince Ivan, and up he came to the old woman's hut. As he entered he saw her winding gold thread around a spindle.

She then locked it in a box and hid the key. But Prince Ivan quickly found the key, opened the box, took out the spindle and broke it as he had been told. All of a sudden, there was Yelena the Fair standing in front of him.

"Oh, Prince Ivan," she sighed, "how long you were in coming! I almost wed another." And Prince Ivan and Yelena the Fair went home and they lived happily ever after.

The Blacksmith's Daughter

Anon

IN A WOODEN HOUSE deep in the forest lived a blacksmith and his daughter. The blacksmith worked hard all day shoeing horses, while his daughter pumped up the fire, carried water from the well, chopped wood, dug the garden, picked fruit from the trees, trimmed the candles and cooked the meals. Her hands were rough and coarse, her face pale with work and little sleep, and her hair matted with dirt. Even so, some men came seeking her hand in marriage.

"What's the good of that?" said the girl, "I won't marry till I find someone I love with all my heart."

One day, the king's messenger came riding through the land to proclaim that the prince of the kingdom had been enchanted by a wicked sorcerer. He was imprisoned in a deep cave sealed with three locks. The king was offering a reward of the greatest treasure in his kingdom to anyone who could rescue the prince. All the young nobles of the land saddled their horses and went off to try their luck.

The next day, the blacksmith's daughter put down her tools and said, "Father, if you can get along without me, I've a mind to try and rescue the prince myself." She had seen a picture of the prince, and it pained her heart that anyone with such a merry face should lie under such an evil enchantment.

So she packed a bundle with some bread, clothes and her tools. She walked through the forest, day after day, sleeping where she could and earning a little money for food, till she came to the place of the enchantment. The king and queen were there, as was the king's messenger, who had proclaimed of the prince's capture.

There stood the greatest wonder she had ever seen — a cave with an iron door three feet thick, with three mighty keyholes. In front of the cave stood three huge pillars, towering into the sky, one of flame, one of ice, and one of wax.

"On the top of each pillar," explained the king's messenger, "is a key to one of the keyholes. But the wax pillar is too smooth to climb, the ice pillar too slippery, and the fire pillar has killed scores of our best knights."

All day the blacksmith's daughter watched as man after man tried their luck. They showed great courage and daring but the three pillars defeated them all. Many were badly hurt, and all were carried away to be tended in the king's tent, for the king and queen watched every attempt, praying for success to free their son.

At last it was the blacksmith's daughter's turn to try.

"Humph," she said. "This is work for

someone who understands work."

She went into the forest with her axe, gathered huge bundles of wood and built an enormous fire around the base of the ice pillar. Next she dug a channel between the ice pillar and the fire pillar. She lit the fire and with her bellows, puffed and puffed until she had a roaring blaze. Steadily, slowly, the ice began to melt. At first it dripped slowly but soon the water rained down in torrents, and the pillar dwindled and dwindled. As the ice melted, the water gathered in the channel she had dug and ran down to the pillar of flame. It surged against the pillar and the fires at the bottom died away with a hiss. The whole pillar slowly collapsed downwards.

As it fell, the key from the top of it shot into the grass where the blacksmith's daughter snatched it up. At the same moment, the ice pillar dwindled to a height where she could finally reach up to seize the key from its top.

Only the pillar of wax was left. She scooped up a great shovelful of hot coals from the pillar of flames, and spread them at the base of the pillar of wax.

The heat softened the wax just enough to allow her to carve out small holes, like steps, in its side. Putting her foot into the first hole and quickly cutting another one for her hand,

28

she started to climb. Up she went, steadily cutting holes with her hand axe. When she reached the top, there lay the third key. She picked it up and climbed swiftly down, for the wax was becoming dangerously soft, and dripped around her.

As she slid to the ground, a cheer went up, and the king himself rose from his platform and came forward. The three keys were fitted to the locks and out came the prince.

His gaze fell on the blacksmith's daughter. The ice water had washed the dust and dirt from her hair, the fire had put colour in her cheeks and the wax had softened her hands. The prince could not take his eyes off her.

"You deserve any reward you care to claim, even to half my kingdom," said the king. "Name it and it shall be yours."

The blacksmith's daughter said simply,

"Your majesty offered as a reward his greatest treasure. Is not the prince himself your greatest treasure?"

"Do you mean?" asked the queen, but the eyes of the prince and the blacksmith's daughter had spoken without words, and each knew what the other wanted. The prince drew her to him, the king signalled his approval and the people gave a cheer. They knew one day the prince would be their king and it would be useful to have a queen who knew how things worked.

The Goose Girl

By the Brothers Grimm

A QUEEN HAD A BEAUTIFUL DAUGHTER, who was going to be married to a young prince of a neighbouring kingdom. It was arranged that she was to travel to his country accompanied by her maid. The queen provided the princess with many beautiful robes and jewels, and gave her a wonderful horse named Falada, which had the amazing gift of speech.

Just before the princess started on her journey, the queen pricked her finger, and dropped three drops of blood upon a handkerchief. "Take this my dear," she told her daughter. "It will serve you if you are ever in danger."

They shed many tears at parting, but at last the princess mounted Falada and started on the journey.

When she and the maid had ridden for some time, they came to a stream of clear water. The princess asked the

maid to bring her a drink of water, but the girl replied rudely that she could get the water for herself.

The princess dismounted and drank from the stream, but as she raised her head the handkerchief bearing the three drops of blood fell from her dress and floated down the stream. The maid noticed and was very pleased. Without the three drops of

blood, the princess was completely in her power, and the nasty servant immediately forced the princess to exchange her royal dress for her own servant's one.

After making her promise never to betray the terrible secret, the maid mounted Falada and left her own horse for the princess. Falada took the false princess to the palace, and when they arrived the prince came out to meet them, and took the false bride to the royal chamber. The true bride had followed on the maid's horse, and was left in the court below. Seeing her there, forlorn and beautiful, the king inquired who she was.

"Only my servant," the false bride carelessly replied. "Give her some work to keep her busy."

So the king sent the true princess to help a boy called Curdken herd geese — and so it happened that the real bride became a goose girl.

One day shortly after, the false bride remembered Falada's gift of speech and became worried he might give her away. She told the prince that the horse was vicious, and that she wished its head to be cut off. The prince, having no reason to doubt her, at once carried out her orders.

When the real princess heard the sad news, she dried her tears and sought the executioner. She could not save her dear Falada from his doom, but she persuaded him to place the horse's head over the great gate through which she had to pass on her way to the goose pasture.

The next morning, when she and Curdken drove their geese under the gate, the princess cried, "O Falada, hang you there?" And to

the princess's astonishment the horse head at
once replied to her,

"'Tis Falada, Princess fair.

   If she knew this, for your sake

   Your mother's heart would break."

When she had driven the geese to the
field, the princess sat down and let her
golden hair down.

The sun shone upon it, and Curdken
caught at its golden threads and tried to pull
one out as a keepsake but the goose girl
called to the wind,

"Wind, blow gently here, I pray,

   And take Curdken's hat away.

   Keep him chasing o'er the world,

   While I bind my hair of gold."

The wind did as she asked, and Curdken
ran so far for his hat that when he returned
the golden hair was plaited and bound

about her head. Curdken was cross all day long, and when at night they had driven the geese home, he complained to the king.

"The goose girl so teases me that I will no longer herd the geese with her."

When asked how she had offended him, he told the king that she spoke every morning to the horse's head that was over the gate, and that the head replied and called her princess. When morning came the king arose early and stood in the shadow of the town gate. He heard the goose girl say, "O Falada, hang you there?" And he heard the head answer.

Then the king followed on to the field, where he hid behind a bush and watched them herd the geese.

After a time the goose girl undid her glittering hair, and as Curdken snatched at it, the king heard her call the wind again.

The wind came at her bidding, and carried the boy's hat across the fields while she combed her shining hair and fastened it in place.

The king quietly returned to the palace, and that night he sent for the goose girl. He told her he had watched her at the gate and in the field, and asked her the meaning of her strange actions.

"I may not tell, for I swore that if my life was spared I would speak to no one of my woes," she replied.

The king pleaded with her, but she was firm, and at last he told her to tell her troubles to the iron stove, since she would not confide in him. When he had left her, she fell upon her knees before the stove and poured forth her sorrows.

The Goose Girl

"Here am I, the daughter of a queen, doomed to be a goose girl, while the maid steals my treasures and my bridegroom."

She sobbed until the king, who had stood outside and heard all, came in and told her to dry her eyes. He ordered her to dress in royal robes, and she looked beautiful. The prince was summoned, and the old king told him the story. He showed the prince the true bride. He knelt at her feet in admiration, and knew

39

her to be the real princess. When the wicked maid had been punished, the princess was married to the young prince, and reigned with him for many happy years over the kingdom where she had first served as a goose girl.